In loving memory of
Logan James Andersen

— C.T.

Text © 2021 Chris Tougas
Illustrations © 2021 Josée Bisaillon

Published in Canada and the U.S. by Kids Can Press Ltd.
25 Dockside Drive, Toronto, ON M5A 0B5

Kids Can Press is a Corus Entertainment Inc. company

www.kidscanpress.com

The artwork in this book was rendered digitally.
The text is set in Stone Informal.

Edited by Jennifer Stokes
Designed by Barb Kelly

Printed and bound in Shenzhen, China, in 10/2020 by Imago

CM 21 0 9 8 7 6 5 4 3 2 1

Library and Archives Canada Cataloguing in Publication

Title: Poem in my pocket / by Chris Tougas ; illustrated by Josée Bisaillon.

Names: Tougas, Chris, author. | Bisaillon, Josée, illustrator.

Identifiers: Canadiana 20200235923 | ISBN 9781525301452 (hardcover)

Classification: LCC PS8589.O6774 P64 2021 | DDC jC811/.54 — dc23

Kids Can Press gratefully acknowledges that the land on which our office is located is the traditional territory of many nations, including the Mississaugas of the Credit, the Anishnabeg, the Chippewa, the Haudenosaunee and the Wendat peoples, and is now home to many diverse First Nations, Inuit and Métis peoples.

We thank the Government of Ontario, through Ontario Creates; the Ontario Arts Council; the Canada Council for the Arts; and the Government of Canada for supporting our publishing activity.

To Martin, the king of puns

— J.B.

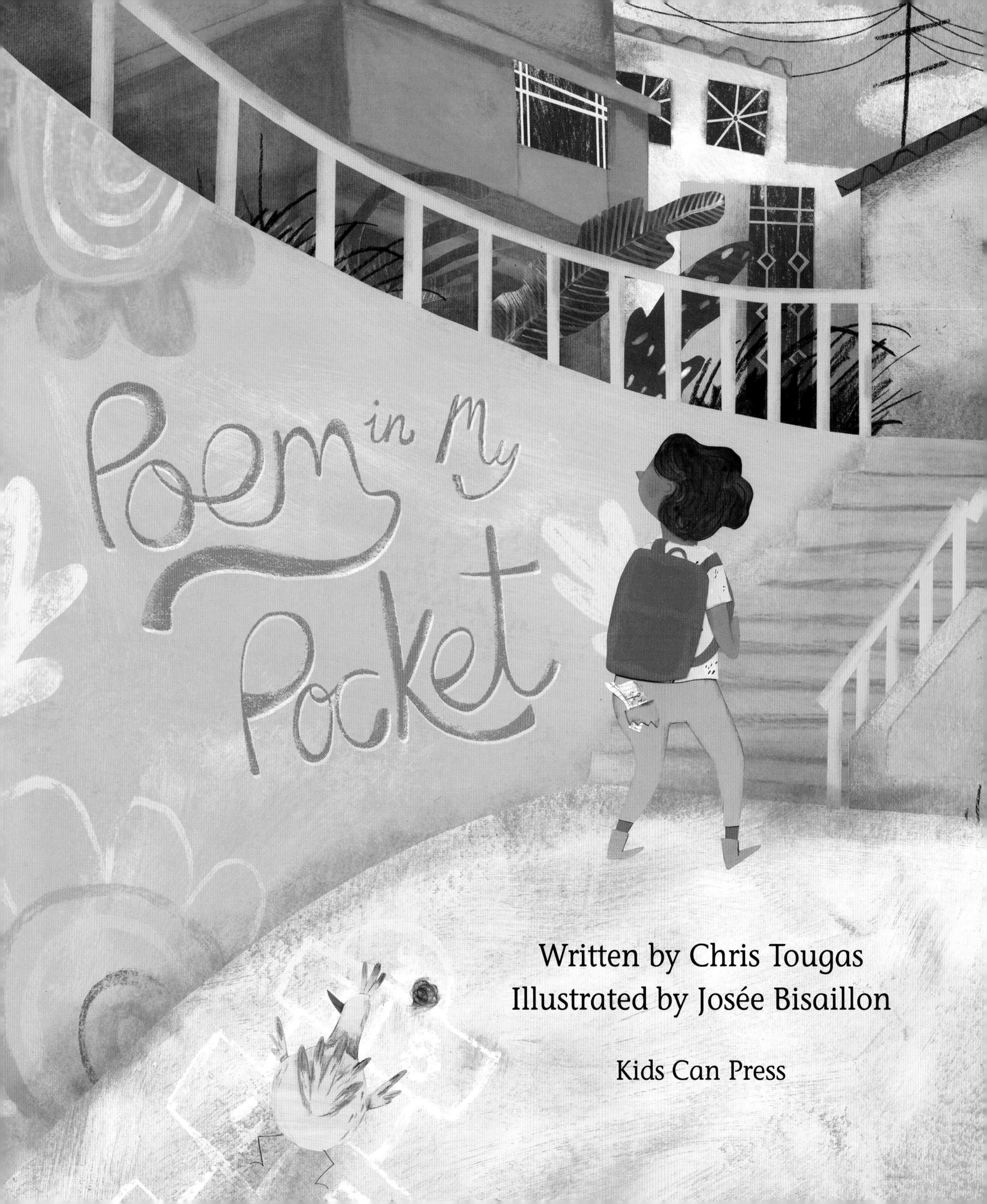

Poem in My Pocket

Written by Chris Tougas

Illustrated by Josée Bisaillon

Kids Can Press

I had a poem in my pocket,
but my pocket got a rip.
Rhymes tumbled down my leg
and trickled from my hip.

word

write

slide

ride

Slipping, sliding, dipping, diving,
rhythms hit the ground.
Then ...
a whirling, twirling, swirling wind
blew all my rhymes around!

Scribbled thoughts were scattered —
there were letters here and there.
Mixed-up words were whipped about
and mingled in midair.

WILL YOU M ME?

eow-y

B
B
B beautiful!

Big and little letters
formed some super silly puns.
Playful words made playful rhymes.
Their fun had just begun!

MOVING ON!
COMPANY
Beep Beep
Beep

Anything
is
POPSICLE!

I gathered poem pieces,
but I couldn't make them fit.
I tried to recreate my verse.
I couldn't remember it!

balloon

motion
fantastic cat
umbrella
flower
tomatoes
beautiful

My poem was a puzzle.
I reworked my words, but then …
a whirling, twirling, swirling wind
blew them away — again!

watermelon

wind

fan

heart

book

Thunder clouds came rolling in.
The rain came pouring down,
mixing all my magic words
into the muddy ground.

Stuff

head

bag

feather

ear

kites

talk

heart

need

smell

love

The seeds of thoughts were planted.

I had set my story free!

That poem in my pocket

turned into a ...

POETREE!

DID YOU FIND these rhyming words?

Page 4 and 5
groove/move	fun/sun
bird/word	write/right
slide/ride	

Page 6 and 7

mat/hat	wet/pet
rip/whip	pop/hop
big/dig	race/face
shoe/blew	mouse/house

Page 22 and 23
letter/better	
believe/achieve	
book/look	start/smart
brain/gain	rhyme/time
read/seed	print/hint
spell/tell	art/heart
learn/yearn	find/mind
form/storm	create/great
sing/ring	flow/grow

DID YOU FIND these mixed-up words?

Page 8 and 9
laundry	umbrella	cloud	cactus
sweep	flower	window	bird
tree	balloon	ladder	cat

Poem in My Pocket Day

Every April during National Poetry Month, one day is set aside as **Poem in Your Pocket Day.** People participate by choosing a poem, carrying it with them throughout the day and sharing it with others.

Visit the following websites for more information:

www.poets.org/national-poetry-month/poem-your-pocket-day

www.poets.ca/pocketpoem/